I Promise

For David Peter,
son of Babette and Patrick,
with love from U.D.

About This Book

This book was edited by Andrea Spooner and Deirdre Jones and designed by Phil Caminiti and Becca Dunn with art direction by Sasha Illingworth. The production was supervised by Erika Schwartz, and the production editors were Barbara Bakowski and Jen Graham. The illustrations for this book were done in pen and ink and watercolor on Arches cold-pressed watercolor paper. The text was set in Stempel Garamond, and the display type was hand-lettered by David Coulson.

• Little, Brown and Company • Hachette Book Group • 1290 Avenue of the Americas, New York, NY 10104 • Visit us at lb-kids.com • Little, Brown and Company is a division of Hachette Book Group, Inc. • The Little, Brown name and logo are trademarks of Hachette Book Group, Inc. • The publisher is not responsible for websites (or their content) that are not owned by the publisher. • First Edition: March 2017 • Library of Congress Cataloging-in-Publication Data • Names: McPhail, David, 1940– author, illustrator. • Title: I promise / David McPhail. • Description: First edition. | New York : Little, Brown and Company, 2017. | Summary: A little bear learns from his mother what it means to make and break a promise, as well as the lesson that some things in life simply cannot be promised. • Identifiers: LCCN 2015028882 | ISBN 9780316297875 (hardcover) • Subjects: | CYAC: Promises—Fiction. | Bears—Fiction. | Mother and child—Fiction. • Classification: LCC PZ7.M478818 Iam 2017 | DDC [E]—dc23 • LC record available at http://lccn.loc.gov/2015028882 • 10 9 8 7 6 5 4 3 2 1 • APS • PRINTED IN CHINA

I Promise

David McPhail

Little, Brown and Company

New York   Boston

Baby Bear and his mother were splashing in the pool below the waterfall.

"Will you sing to me, Momma?" shouted Baby Bear over the roar of the falling water.

"Later, dear," Mother Bear shouted back. "I promise!"

"What's a promise?" Baby Bear asked as they sat in the sun, drying off.

"A promise is when you say you will do something," answered Mother Bear, "and then do your very best to do it."

"But what if you don't do it?" said Baby Bear.

"Then it becomes a *broken* promise."

"Can you fix it?" asked Baby Bear.

"Not easily," said his mother. "That's why it's so important to keep it."

Baby Bear was quiet for a moment.

Then he said, "I told Billy Bear I would play with him tomorrow. If I don't, is that breaking a promise?"

"What do you think?" his mother replied.

"Yes," said Baby Bear. "I think it is. And that might hurt Billy Bear's feelings."

"I think you are right, Baby Bear."

Mother and Baby Bear got up and walked along the riverbank.

"What *else* do you promise, Momma?" Baby Bear asked.

"I promise to lie in the meadow with you," said Mother Bear, "and watch the clouds float by."

"Maybe we will see one that looks like an elephant!" Baby Bear said excitedly. "What else do you promise?"

"I promise to listen when you have something to tell me," said Mother Bear.

"Like when I told you I thought there was a dragon under my bed?" Baby Bear asked.

"Yes, exactly," replied Mother Bear. "I remember that we *looked*, but we didn't find anything."

"And you stayed with me until I fell asleep," said Baby Bear. "Just in case."

"That's what mothers do," his mother told him.

They walked down to the orchard, where the apples were nearly ripe. Mother Bear shook some from the tree. "What else do you promise?" Baby Bear asked her.

"I promise to give you good things to eat," said Mother Bear,
"so that you will grow up to be big and strong."

"Will I be as big as *you*, Momma?" Baby Bear asked.

"Oh, yes, dear," said Mother Bear. "Maybe even bigger!"

"Will you sing to me *now*?" Baby Bear asked.

"Not now, dear," mumbled his mother, her mouth full of apple. "Later. I promise."

After a while, they walked toward the deep woods.

"What else do you promise?" Baby Bear asked.

"I promise to teach you the things you will need to know about growing up," said Mother Bear. "But I also promise to let you discover some things for yourself. I don't know *everything*!"

"You don't?" said Baby Bear, sounding surprised.

"I don't," his mother replied. "No one knows *all* there is to know."

"Do you promise I will always be happy?" Baby Bear asked.

"Oh, I can't promise you *that*!" said his mother. "Your happiness will depend mostly on *you*. But I will do everything I can to help."

Now they were on the path that led home. The sun had set, and the moon was rising.

"Do you promise anything else?" Baby Bear asked.

"I promise I will love you," said Mother Bear, "always and forever!"

"No matter what?" Baby Bear asked.

"No matter what!" Mother Bear promised.

Baby Bear was very tired, so Mother Bear picked him up and carried him the rest of the way home.

"I can't wait to see Billy Bear tomorrow," said Baby Bear. "I'm glad I promised to play with him."

"That must feel good," said Mother Bear. "You will be keeping your promise and having fun, too!"

When they reached their den, Mother Bear laid
Baby Bear down on his bed and tucked him in.

"Can I promise *you* something, Momma?" Baby Bear asked.

"Of course, dear," said Mother Bear. "What is it?"

"I promise I will be a good bear…" Baby Bear told her, "most of the time."

"*Most of the time* will do nicely," said Mother Bear.
Then she sang to her baby until he was sound asleep.

"Good night, Baby Bear."